Courbee' Exotica: *The Art of Seduction*

Welcome to Courbee' Exotica premiere issue Spring 2020!

There are over 14 billion Plus Size women (sizes 8 to 28) all over the world. Historically, we have been ignored, marginalized, teased, and out casted by society, social media, fashion designers, film producers, casting directors, advertisers, fashion industry, and Hollywood.

Plus Size Women are 14 billion strong global. Although the average size is 14/16, we have far and few celebrations for PSW as beautiful, intelligent, sexy, and being a seductress.

Plus Size talent is slowly emerging to the runways of New York, Milan, and Paris. Moreover, television and other media are slowly but surely embracing Courbee' Revolucion' or the size women.

Fat shaming, bullying, sexual assault, and the marginalization of women has come to a fast halt with the #Metoo, #TimesUp, and #NoMore movements. We add to those movements: the Plus Size Revolution known as Courbee'Exotica.'

In this cutting-edge pictorial, each page is seduction at its best. The "Art of Seduction" consist of a unique array of photographers and Plus Size Models from all over the United States and Canada.

This pictorial has the trajectory sexuality fantasy and reality intertwine in each image. It is a quintessential perspective of Plus Size Women that has never been immortalize on this level. We have level up, and the visions of Plus Size Models have been capture in their true naturally form.

Regardless if you did or did not like the Ms. Sidibe's love scene, Courbee' Revolucion' Exotica will give you more to talk about. While this is an certainly an opportunity for Plus Size Women sexuality to be put in the forefront with a positive light, it is not a dirty shameful secret that Plus Size Women have beautiful bodies and there is no shame in our game!

Courbee' Exotica:
The Art of Seduction

We emphasize the art of exoticism and seductresses, because the true art of a women's sexuality is to leave much to the imagination. The subtleness of "the look", twinkle in the eye, a suddenly smile, the slight twist of the neck, or a bashful nod. It is exotica at it's best.

In this publication, we celebrate the Plus Size Woman who has truly embrace her authentic self by knowing – she is enough. By the way, yes Plus Size Women have sex and plenty of it!

I hope enjoy our vision pictorials of beautiful women of all shapes, sizes, and ethnicity. We hope to inspire women who believe that they are not enough, whatever reason to know that, you are more than enough.

We celebrate that you are perfectly, wonderfully, and awesomely created by God.

You Have a Choyce
Always Share Love!

JAMILA JAY, LOS ANGELES, CA
Dress Size 16 Height 5'9–

Yolanda "Yo-Yo" Whitaker
Hip Hop ICON & LIVING LEGEND
The True Women Empowerment Movement – The Hip Hop Movement

The true Women Empower is the process of empowering women financially, socially, emotionally, and economically. Moreover, for women of color, it is defined as empowering our communities and families by any and all means necessary. Decades later, in 2017 and 2018, the #Me-too (against sexual harassment and assault), and #Times up's movement (celebrities untied against Weinstein) exploded across the entertainment world.

Women Empowerment & the Ladies of Hip Hop

In the late 1980s and early 1990s, they were the quintessential originators and innovators that mandated the foundation for the Women's Empowerment Movement. There was a need for women to become self-empowered, and it influenced the foundational of female rap artists. The lyrics had an empowering message with a feminist twist combined with a strong hook and electrifying beat. The beats consisted of reggae, R&B, soul, and funk. This genre of music changed the quality of life for women globally and it changed the trajectory of Rap music!

This became the anthem for empowerment and change. The music depicted strong Black Women (It's me the brand new intelligent black woman Y-O-Y-O) who tackled social issues of domestic violence, infidelities, and drug usage. While demanding respect (Who you calling a bitch?) and uplifting the Black Man!

(U-N-I-T-Y Uh, U.N.I.T.Y., U.N.I.T.Y. that's a unity U.N.I.T.Y., love a black man from infinity to infinity)

Living Legends and Icons – Female Rappers

In 1984, living legends and icon Lolita Gooden aka Roxanne Shante changed the rap game. As a young female rapper from the Queensbridge housing project in Queens, NYC, she battled male rappers in her neighborhood. She recorded her seven-minute freestyle over UTFO's 1984 song.

In 1988, Dana Elaine Owens, known professionally as Queen Latifah, from Newark, New Jersey, signed a record deal with Tommy Boy Records.

Another living legend in the Hip-hop genre is Lana Michelle Moorer, professionally know as MC Lyte. In 1988, at only 17 years of age, she is an American rapper who first gained fame in the late 1980s. She became the first solo female rapper to release a full album entitled "Lyte as a Rock MC Lyte." She released her first song, a political and empowering tune, "I Cram to Understand U (Sam)." It was about the crack epidemic and its impact on relationships.

In 1993, Queen Latifah UNITY shattered on the airwaves with powerful lyrics and reggae beat, "U-N-I-T-Y Uh, U.N.I.T.Y., U.N.I.T.Y. that's a unity-U.N.I.T.Y., love a black man from infinity to infinity."

Roxanne Shante, Queen Latifah, and MC Lyte represented the East Coast, but on the West Coast, we had the amazing "Yo-Yo. On the West Coast, we had the amazing "Yo-Yo." Similarly to her East Coast counterparts, she empowered females with her lyrical, social consciousness track, "You Can't Play with my Yo-Yo."

In 1991, she exploded musically with a mantra of Women's Empowerment, self-pride, and mandating respect with culturally explosive lyrists: "It's me the brand new intelligent black woman Y-O-Y-O Which is YO, YO but I'm not too played like I was made by Mattel, But this Yo-Yo- was made by women and male...."

She represented the sisters from Northern and Southern California: from East Oakland to Sacramento and the Southern California cities of South Central, Compton, and Inglewood. She was one of us, but the women worldwide related to this lyricist. Women globally who were disfranchised drenched with pain and despair song, "Don't try to play me out, don't try to play me out."

> But this Yo-Yo is made by woman and male
> I rhyme about uprights up liftin the woman
> For that are superior to handle by any male
> Any time, any rhyme, any flow, and any show
> And if you ask my producers that we fly and you know....

YOLANDA "YO-YO" WHITAKER is a Grammy-nominated rapper, actress, educator, philanthropist, and entrepreneur. She has been blessed with many accolades and awards, but her most important achievements are her two beautiful and intelligent daughters and a new grandbaby. Her music has illuminated her stance on female empowerment while denouncing the sexism found in the hip-hop genre. Yo-Yo named her crew the Intelligent Black Woman's Coalition (IBWC).

The Interview – She is gracious and kind. It seemed like I was just chatting it up with an old friend about women empowerment, body issues, and so much more. YO-YO was very kind and gracious. Her voice had a tonality of excitement about the past, present, and future.

As a Plus-Size advocate, I wanted to know if the beautiful 'Yo-Yo had anybody issues. Living in Southern California, and being in front of the camera as a rapper and actor must be stressful. We can be our worst critic.

I asked, "Were their times when she felt her body was not just right."

She replied, '...all the time. Every time I looked back on pictures I looked at old pictures and say why was I tripping. I was perfect. I continued to look back. Wow, I was perfect."

She continued, 'As a 48 woman in hip hop, I look at my body and say oh, God. I know I need to take the time to work out. It is a mind, body, and soul thing. I feel better when I work out versus what I look like. People say you look great."

In 2020, Women Empowerment and self-acceptance are paramount.

The entertainer, songwriter, actress, & rapper Lizzo has taken the torch of Women Empowerment and self-love (Plus Size)!

I asked Yo-Yo her impression of Grammy Award winner Lizzo. She replied, "I loved her, and my first time hearing her without seeing her I loved her and then seeing her I just admired her. Wow, I get it! That is what music is and that is what success is! Success is finding that happy medium and rolling with it being completely satisfied with what you are doing.

If you only measured it to yourself. I am excited for women, I

am excited about living within your truths. I am excited for people who are Firestarter's.'

YO-YO the ENTREPRENEUR - In 2012-2013, The Schott Foundation for Public Education reported black males in U.S. public schools estimated that 59 percent of black males graduated from high school, compared to 65 percent of Latino males and 80 percent of white males.

In 2012, Yo-Yo was informed about the high school dropout rate especially for Black Boys, she knew that she had to address the plagued that infected her community.

In 2013, she founded the Yo-Yo School of Hip Hop Music Academy where she teaches youth about arts and academics. Since 2012, Yo-Yo's, "How to Get A's in English through Hip Hop," seminar has been a main feature during the expo. With a commitment to educating our youth, Yo-Yo is an Ambassador for the Black College Expo. The expo is an event that highlights over 50 of the 104 historically black colleges and universities.

Can you tell me about Yo-Yo School of Hip Hop? She answered, "Yo-Yo School of Hip Hop is an arts' and academic program. It started as a summer art program. Thanks to Congress Women Maxine Waters who helped us get situated. I just wanted to teach Hip Hop. I wanted to teach Beat production. I wanted to teach Hip Hop lyrics. I wanted everything on the industrial scale. I wanted them to learn exactly how it was to be in the industry, not a talent show level."

She continued, "So that is what I wanted to provide. We had over 100 kids (we had a waiting list of 100 students who wanted to participate. The majority were young black men Demographic (ages) 13- 17. Hip Hop is that powerful." Teaching young black boys how to write by using rap was a successful endeavor.

It was so successful that she decided to conduct research and confer with collegiate scholars and professors who taught Hip Hop and Ebonics on a college level. She comprised her own curriculum "How to get A's through Hip Hop." She conducted workshops, seminars, and courses at the Black College Expos, Schools Seminars College Expo. She said, "It has organically grown."

YO-YO the COMMUNITY ACTIVITIST-Yo-Yo also makes her mark on the airwaves as co-host of Café Mocha, the #1 nationally syndicated radio show for women of color, alongside Emmy award winner Loin Love and broadcast veteran Angelique Perrin. The Gracie award-winning show is heard in over 35 markets across the United States and on Sirius XM Channel 141. Yo-Yo teaches women about health and fitness via her "Get Fit with Yo-Yo" program.

YO-YO & MUSIC - Raised in the infamous South Central district of Los Angeles, her big break came when she appeared on Ice Cube's 1990 debut. As the protégé of rapper, actor, producer, director, and writer Ice Cube, she debuted, on his tracks "AmeriKKKa's Most Wanted," and "It's A Man's World." She represented women and being empowered was clearly depicted in those tracks.

Her own debut "Make Way for the Motherload" introduced her confident attitude along with the formation of the Intelligent Black Women's Coalition organization. Her songs "You Can't Play with My Yo-Yo," "Bonnie & Clyde Theme" with Ice Cube. My favorite was her feature on Brandy's, "I Wanna Be Down," remix with MC Lyte and Queen Latifah. It is a classic.

In the fall of 2019, she released him "Out of Control," her first new song in more than 10 years. The track features "Love & Hip Hop Hollywood" castmate Brittany B, who is also an A&R for Warner Bros., Tyler Reign, season 5 winner of Jermaine Dupri's "Rap Game" series, as well as Patient Picasso.

YO-YO on TELEVISION & MOVIES, 'Yo-Yo" seemly made the transition from music to television and movies. As the newest member of VH1's popular, "Love & Hip Hop Hollywood" series is affectionately known as Auntie Yo-Yo. She is a mentor and role model for the younger aspiring rappers on the show.

As an actress, she has appeared in the Academy Awards-nominated film "Boyz N the Hood" as well as several television shows including '90s sitcom "Martin" where she portrayed the memorable, comical recurring character Keylolo. She also served as a co-host of VH1's "Miss Rap Supreme."

I saluted her as a living legend and icon. I saluted Ms. Whitaker as a female in a male dominate industry who preserved not only did she strive, but thrive. I saluted her as pioneer in the Women Empowerment movement, and I am excited for Yo-Yo and longevity as an entertainer. As I am listened to her single 'Out of Control' on the radio and watching her on 'Love & Hip Hop Hollywood' on VH1. I have to admit she is totally in control in the next phase of her career and life. We applaud you are the West Coast 'Princess of Rap.'

If you would like to view Yo-Yo's videos and listen to her music check out www.skycitydjz.net –FunkFunk radio and go to the Jamila Choyce link.

Written by

Jamila Choyce

JamilaJayPlusSizeCasting@gmail.com

Christa Cora

GLEN RIDGE, NEW JERSEY

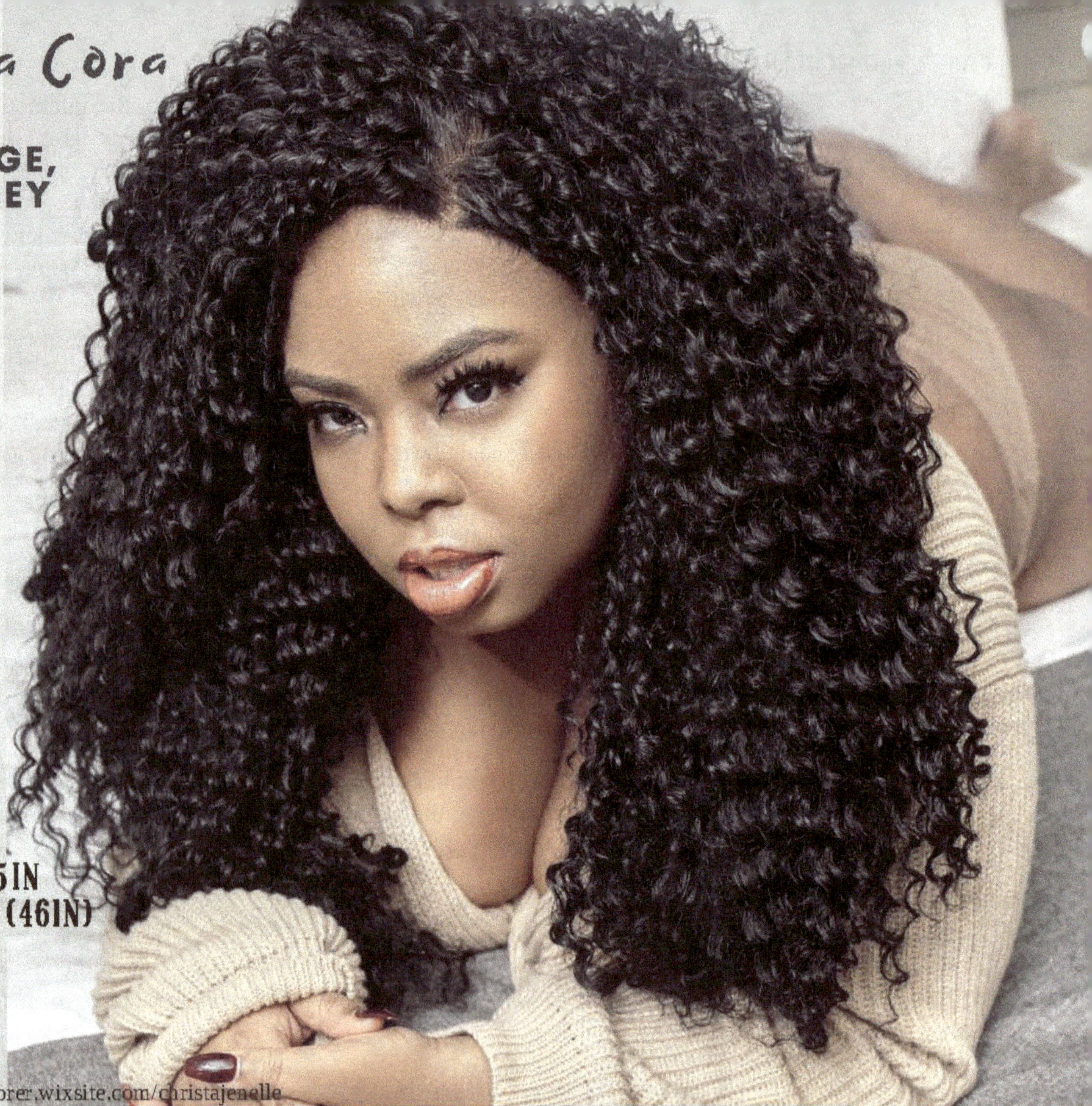

HEIGHT: 5FT5IN
BUST: 42DDD (46IN)
HIPS: 46IN
WAIST: 38IN
SHOE: 8.5

Size: 16/18

Website: coratexplorer.wixsite.com/christajenelle

"JUST BE TRUE TO WHO YOU ARE, NO MATTER WHAT SIZE OR SHAPE YOU MIGHT BE!"

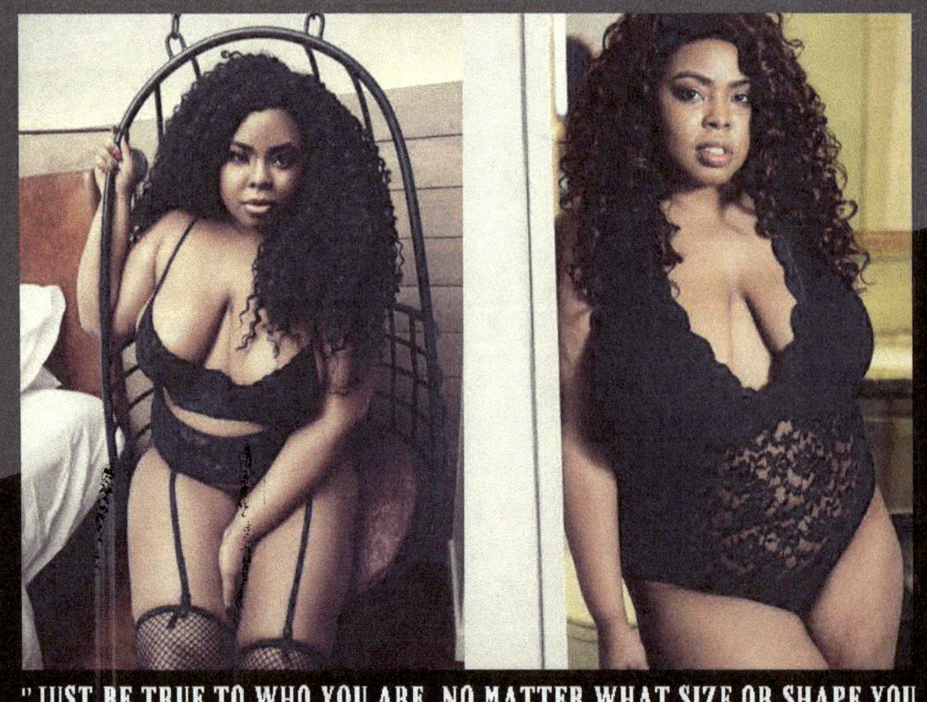

Christa Cora

QUEEN NATASHANay,
Los Angeles, CA

Dress size 16/18   Height 5'8

Height
5'2

Dress Size
20

Shoe size 9.5/1 0

PLUS SIZE MODEL
DR. ALLISON,
SINGLE MOM,
FULL-TIME STUDENT,
EMPLOYED FULL-TIME
PLUS SIZE MODEL,
SINGER, &
ACTRESS

Shadaria Allison
#MARRIED2IT

ATK Curve Weekend
SITUATIONS MEDIA ENTERTAINMENT
102.6 THE [SITUATION]
Online Radio For Everyone
WSTM-DB HD1 ATLANTA-CHARLOTTE
JULY 23-25, 2020
ATLANTA, GA
CURVES OF ELEGANCE GALA--SPLASH BASH--CURVY COOKOUT--CURVEILLANCE
MORE INFO:
WWW.ATLANTACURVEWEEKEND.COM
Made with PosterMyWall.com

L. Llewellyn James

In that capacity, Mr. James works as a Traditional Illustrator, Graphic Designer, 3d Computer Modeling Artist, Documentary Filmmaker and Voice-over Artist.

Mr. James has worked for an eclectic array of clientele, ranging from The Evangelical Lutheran Church in America, The Discovery Museum and Science Planetarium and The African-American Historical Association of Fairfield County, Connecticut.

You can see much more of Mr. James' work as a Filmmaker, Illustrator, Graphic Designer and 3d Computer Modeler via his website at www.alphamediaworks.com

His IG handle is @l_llewellyn_james, while he can be reached on Twitter @AlphaholicOne

JAMEELAH

DRESS SIZE 16   HEIGHT 5'6

"i am" a survivor- "i rock with success"

In 2017, I was diagnosed with high-risk stage 2 breast cancer. Therefore, my platform is breast cancer and cancer awareness. Stage 2 means the breast cancer is growing, but it is still contained in the breast or growth has only extended to the nearby lymph nodes. This stage is divided into groups: Stage 2A and Stage 2B. The difference is determined by the size of the tumor and whether the breast cancer has spread to the lymph nodes.

I am blessed, because many Black Women die from breast cancer. According to the CDC, Black women and white women get breast cancer at about the same rate, but black women die from breast cancer (incidence rates) and higher rates of dying from breast cancer (death rates) between 1999 and 2013. During this period, breast cancer incidence went down among white women, and went up slightly among black women. Now, breast cancer incidence is about the same for women of both races.

Death from breast cancer are going down among both black and white women, especially among younger black women. But breast cancer death rates are 40% higher among black women than white women.

I often ask myself "Why do I think it happened to me?" Cancer seems to a relentless aliment in my family. For example, my immediate family has suffered several deaths. My mother's sister and brother past away a week apart from cancer. My father's sister passed from cancer as well. Cancer seems to be in my DNA on both sides of my family –mother and father.

As for me, I ended up receiving a lumpectomy in my right breast. Lumpectomy is the removal of the breast tumor (the "lump") and some of the normal tissue that surrounds it.

After surgery, I had 5 strong chemo treatments which landed me in the hospital for weeks each time. I decided to stop my doctor from God.

That message was, "I was no longer doing any more chemo." The doctors wanted to give me 12 milder ones, but I told the doctor God said: "...this is it." I did 8 weeks of radiation and ended up with a big open sore under my armpit.

Thank God for Medi-Cal. If it was not for them, who knows what may have happended? My advice to other women is to listen to your body. If it says that it can't tolerate the treatment, try something different. Do not let your body suffer! Please remember to always go get your breasts examined. Always go get check-ups never let a year go by especially if you're high risk like I was.

My motivation now is how can I cange my situation, and that would be to continue to believe in God, trust in his word, and have lots of faith.

I exercise and take good of my body. Most importantly, I keep my mind stress free. At this point, my soul is happy. I am enjoying in my life, and I would not change anything different from waht I went through. That is why I rock with success!

Jameelah Johnson

BROWN SUGA,
OAKLAND,
CALIFORNIA

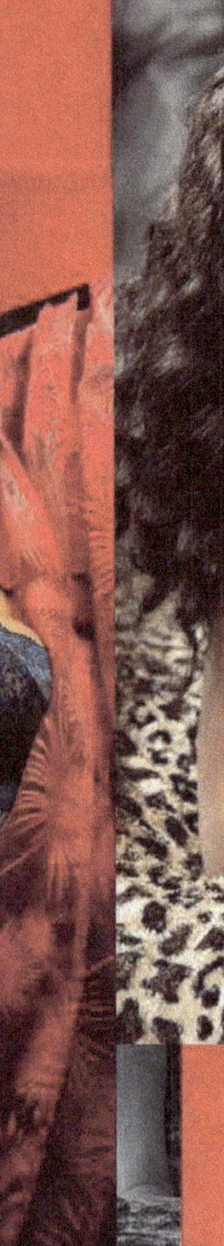

HEIGHT 5'1
DRESS SIZE 12- 1

50 & FABULOUS

50 & FABULOUS - Trina Monique Hearne
"Brown Suga"

Life is Beautiful and I am looking forward to another 50 years of complete bliss with my universal soul mate, family and friends.

I was born Trina Monique Hearne on March 18, 1970. Who knew that I would make an appearance earlier than my April 10 due date, at 4lb-15oz. Yes, I am a preemie.

My parents were married for five years, but after both my parents struggled with substances, abuse and infidelities they divorced in 1975. Due to my mother's illness, I moved around a lot as a child living with friends of the family and relatives.

In my early years, I went to at least six different schools. We finally settled in with my Grandparents and I got to see my dad as often as possible.When I was eight years old, I was molested by a neighbor who was around 16 of age. I didn't understand what that meant then but I knew something was wrong because he told me, '... not to tell anyone."

I believe that couldn't do anything anyway because he was a man. I didn't even tell my dad. After that, I felt like there was nowhere to turn. Somehow I managed to go on in silence for the sake of me and my families safety and well being and eventually blocked it from my memory.

In my neighborhood, I started getting bullied by kids when I was around 9-10 and even by the ones who claimed to be my friends. At one point when I was about 14 years old, I was set up to be jumped by a boy I didn't even know because I wouldn't sleep with him. I thought to myself....... I did not even know you or like you? He busted a blood vessel in my eye, busted my lip, blacked my eye, and crushed my spirit and for what?

After losing my virginity at 16, it threw me into a feeling I had known since I was 8. By 17, I was dating a man who was 25 years old. What in the hell was I thinking? I was almost 18 and smelling myself. If my mother had not been suffering from mental illness, it would have not been possible for me to conduct myself in this type of behavior. I was a teen and running with it.

I was pregnant at 18. Oh Lord, I thought my mother was going to beat this baby out of me. She was upset and very disappointed. But the thing that killed me the most was thinking that people at church would have something to say. That was my first abortion. He was with me, and even took care of me after the procedure, but He wasn't shit. We won't even get into That right now.(Smh).

After Graduating High School at McClymonds High in Oakland California.   I joined the Navy and took up Culinary Arts where I spent the next 13 years of my life. In October 1991, I give birth to my only child, a daughter, T'Schaye Monique.

Between 1991-1997, I met some of my best friends, gained a lot of big and little sisters and gained some family. I found real love and lost it. i traveled the World and the seven seas. After leaving the military in 1999 , I went on to work for the Sheriffs Department, *Nummi*, and the Department of Veterans Affairs.

The past 5 years have been difficult. I lost both my parents and that feeling of emptiness is hard to fill , but I do my best to go on everyday. I suffer from PTSD, depression. and anxiety.   I know that those things are no who I am, but affect only a part of me.

I'm not sure what plans the world has for me, but I am counting on my Ancestors, Universe, and Cosmic Positive Energy to comfort, protect and guide me into a *Life of Abundance, Prosperity, Love* and *Peaceful Journeys*. A life which is lovingly, physically, mentally, emotionally, and spiritually balanced.

Today, I get to enjoy my retirement and spend time with the two of the most important little people in my life, my Sugar Babies. I call them Khaiy Reign, and Kheon Rulez. Life is Beautiful and I am looking forward to another 50 years of complete bliss with my universal soul mate, family and friends.

 I am whole.. Everything I need I shall, have and everything I want shall be given!

TRINA 'Brown Sugr' HEARN FIFTY & FABULOUS

Courbee' Couture Intimate Apparel

A Division of Jamila Jay Fashions

JAMILAJAYPLUSSIZE.com

Dress size 18/20
Height 5'10
Shoe size 11

WASHINGTON, D.C.

Dress Size:18
Stats: 5'8
48G-39-53

"FASHIONISTA
IS FOR
EVERYONE!
I RESPECT
VOGUE AND
FASHION!"
I AM...
SHAY REESE G

JAI,
Los Angeles,
California

Dress Size
14/16
Height 5'8

COLORS
ARE LOVE !

Poohnana
Full Figured Model
Los Angeles,
California

•Height – 5' 6"
•Dress Size – 18
•8 1/2 in shoe size

Mica
San Jose,
California
Dress Size
16/18
Height: 5'9

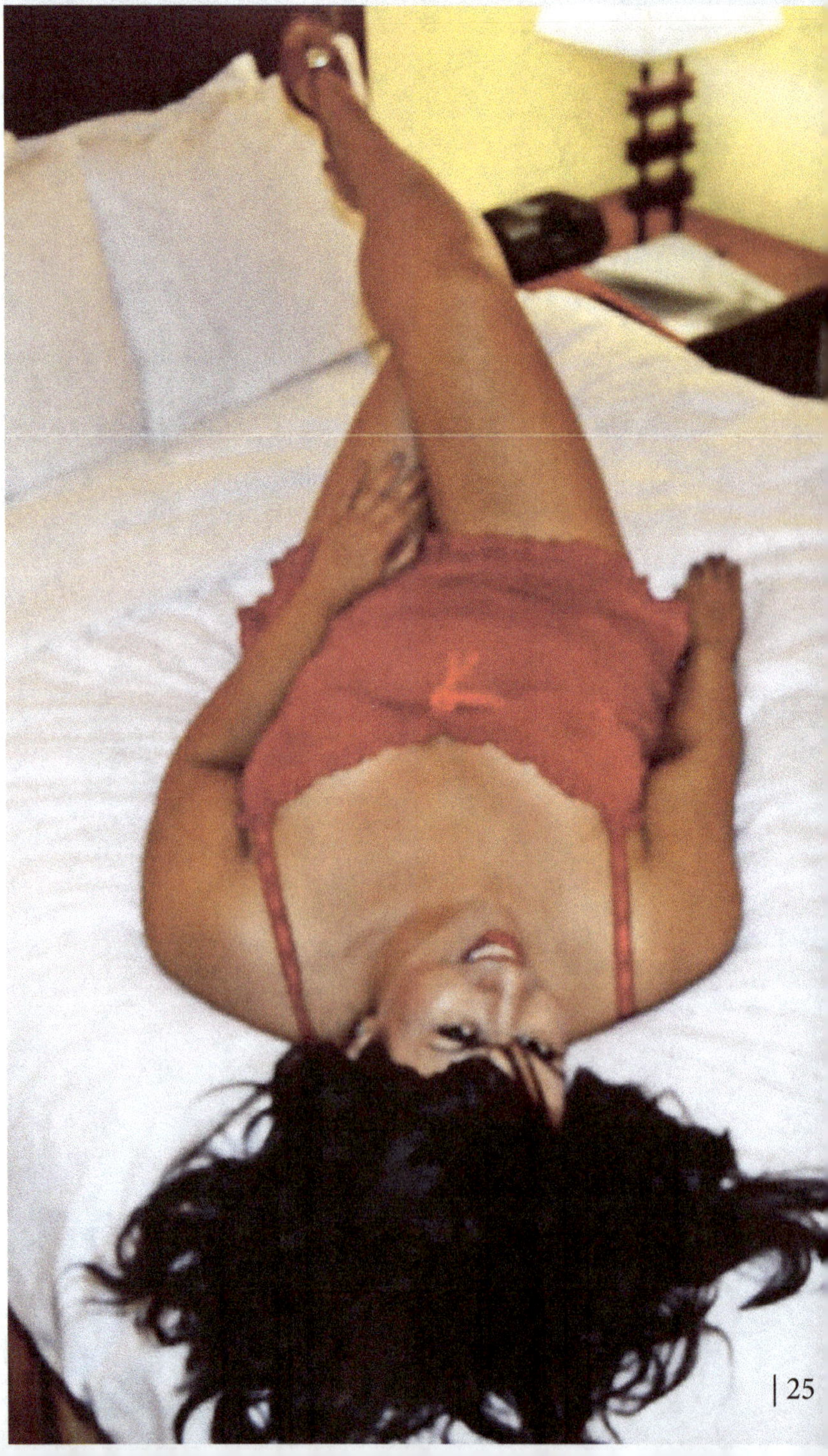

Renee Marie
Vallejo, California
BE YOUR OWN KIND OF BEAUTIFUL
Dress size 18/20   Renee Marie   Height 5'10
Photographer MKi Photography

My body is a Master Piece

Sue Wong McFadden, Durham, North Carolina

Plus Size
Talent

JAMILA JAY
Plus Size
CASTING

JAMILA JAY PlusSizeCasting.com

YOU HAVE A CHOYCE

Experienced or
Aspiring! PlusSizeTalent &
Casting Directors, Models
Calls, Editors, Bloggers, Radio,
& Television
PlusSize Models, Dancers,
Actresses, & Comedians.
www.JamilaJayPlussizecasting.com

LADOM STYLEZZ
OAKLAND, CALIFORNIA

PHOTOGRAPHER
MKI PHOTOGRAPHER

"The Dream is Free, but the Hustle is Sold Separately."
La Dom

Height 5'5
Dress Size 14/16 or XL

MODEL - THE BLACK VICKEYLynn

PLUS SIZE MODELS & SOCIAL MEDIA

Social Media and Plus Size Modeling:
Staying Systematically Social!
Written by
Jamila Choyce, MPA

Staying Systematically Social mean have a method to your social media madness. Each photograph and every post has to be a core meaning or truth, positive, and an aspiring message for you and to others!

Social media is the equivalent of your digital agent that presents your portfolio to the world 24/7! It is your digital portfolio, and your model/actor resume. It is your memory resource, time keeper, and digital document of your triumphs and achievements. This force called social media has with enough mega power to evaluate your career and open doors globally. Plus Size Models like Ashley Graham and Tess "Munster" Holiday used social media to elevate their career into the stratosphere.

Plus size model or not be careful about your post on social media, because if you make it into the local or national news it is the first place the news media will look at. Moreover, do not forget when you land your dream position, guess who is viewing your social pages as a part of a backgound check. If you are turnt up or getting lit - you should be very careful about what you post. Stay Systematically Social on Social Media.

Since the early 2000's; casting directors have been searching social media and peeking at selfies for a rising star. More and more model searches, model casting calls, and bookings are displayed and casted on social media.

In retrospect, I remembered when the classic designer Marc Jacobs made waves when he announced that he would be casting his fall/winter 14 campaign directly through social media, inviting undiscovered stars to tag their tip-top selfies with #castemarc. Marc Jacobs was not the first designer to scout the World Wide Web for talent, but he did embark upon a new vision and conceptual ideas on casting models. He was on the cutting edge of scouting talent which now seems to be the norm.

Quintessentially, social media is a great tool for exposure in the United States and globally. Facebook, Instagram, LinkedIn, Tumblr, and Twitter are just a few social media outlets. However, as a Plus Size Model, the sexual attention can be overwhelming. The likes and the positive comments can be addicting to some models, but never sell your soul for a like!

As the talent, remember to use social media in a way that benefits you. Never forget that, it is your agent, casting director, your professional portfolio, and a reflection of your images as art. That can be easily assesseable to anyone, and it will always remain in cyberspace.

Do not allow yourself to get caught up in the social media frenzy by fueling your photos to appease certain members of your fan base. When I say in a way to benefit you, it means to network with other models, photographers, magazine editors, talent agencies, fashion show directors, and casting officials. More importantly, potential customers.

Moreover I personally have witnessed models getting caught up the frenzy by fueling your photos to appease certain members of your fan base. When I say in a way to benefit you, it means to network with other models, photographers, magazine editors, talent agencies, fashion show directors, and casting officials. More importantly, potential customers.

Social media is an excellent tool for models to market themselves, and to connect with model scouts, talent agents', and casting directors, but you have to stay focus and be true to yourselves. Remember models are defined as "Live Mannequins" at the end of the day, it is your job as a model is to sale a product, brand ambassador, or spokesperson meaning your image is EVERYTHING. It is not about how beautiful you are, or your beautiful hair. You have to sell a product, a concept, or a lifestyle! Stay Systematically Social on Social Media.

As a casting offical, I do not want to see photos of your family, friends, or food on your model page! Remember the three - F's. I only want to see quality upscale photos of you!

Construct a separate social media persona for modeling, and a separate email account. Also, I would choose an alias, because you do not want any stalkers Googling your name and locate your home address.

Many models view social media as a numbers game, but it is really about the images, and the messages you convey. It is about the quality of your content and photos, not the quantity. When your numbers are a high as 60, 000 plus, you may be able to get endorsements or a brand ambassador deal.

Remember the three P's: Persistence, Perseverance, and Patience.

See you on the Runway!

Jamila Choyce

JamilaJayPlusSizeCasting@gmail.com

www.JamilaJayPlusSizeCasting.com

Here is my social media info:

FB: JamilaJayPlusSizeCasting

Intagram: @JamilaChoyce

LinkedIn: Jamila Jay Plus Size Revolution

Twitter: Jamila Choyce

MY BODY IS ART!

Rae Nicole
Baltimore,
Maryland

Dress size 14/16
Height 5'10

Author Brian Jay Nelson – Branchview Series

When paranormal writer Steven Spencer is supernaturally beckoned through his computer to visit a sprawling Connecticut estate, an investigative assignment turns into a life-changing experience. During the inquiry, mysterious spirits of the underworld are exposed. Before Steven has a chance to tell Loraine his life partner, she is also summoned to the Branchview Estate.

The flurry of incidents becomes too much for the couple to handle, and suddenly deceased Jack Branch appears to assist Steven in understanding the happenings. Where soon they find themselves in an epic battle with the elite globalist called the Secret Society.

Will Steven, Loraine, and the others ever get a reprieve from this seemingly endless fight? Will the Secret Society finally be defeated? Will America survive the turmoil, and will the evil ones finally pay the debt for their crimes? All answers lie within the pages of the ongoing saga of the magical, mystical world of Branchview.

When paranormal writer Steven Spencer is supernaturally beckoned through his computer to visit the sprawling Connecticut estate, an investigative assignment turns into a life-changing experience. Once at the Branchview estate, Steven agrees to help the family with a sudden rash of spiritual activity within the house, and a chain reaction of events trail in which his fellow author and life partner, Loraine, is also mysteriously beckoned to help. The ethereal magic within the Great House causes them to realize the deep love they harbor, and they promptly decide to seal it with marriage. In the meantime, Steven comes to learn that he is the illegitimate son of the family matriarch, Penelope Locke Branch. He and Loraine also learn the problems within the house are attributed to a spirit witch who has plagued the family for centuries. Simultaneously, they also find themselves caught in an ongoing feud with a group of wealthy, elite globalists called the Secret Society, who are trying to steal the family's business and their fortune, while also plotting on a much larger scale to destroy, and conquer the United States.

The flurry of incidents that ensue, along with ongoing complications within the Great House, proves too much for Steven and Loraine to handle alone. The spirit of Steven's father, Jack Branch, telepathically summons help from the immortal Mermaid goddess Amphitrite, who secretly walks on land as Dr. Amy Seagraves. They also enlist the help of Dr. Sheila Grayson, a Grand Practitioner of White Magic, and Loraine's former mentor. When the Spirit Witch forms an alliance with the Secret Society, and Hades, the immortal god of the underworld, all hell literally breaks loose. The gods Poseidon and Zeus join the alliance of good, against their brother, and the other forces of evil. Tensions build, and culminate into an epic battle on the historic beach of Lighthouse Point, while a powerful hurricane is churning just offshore. In the midst of some surprising twists and turns, Hades and the Spirit Witch are defeated, but the victory is short-lived, and bittersweet. The aftermath spurned a devastating earthquake and tsunami to the world encompassing Branchview, causing further crisis for its inhabitants, as well as those in the nearby town of Lockeport.

With most of the adult lineage of the Branch family having been killed off by the witch, Steven now stood as the rightful heir to the Branch fortune. He and Loraine continue to fight with their team of Patriot allies against the relentless, and ever powerful forces of the Secret Society, who threaten the future of the Estate, Branch Consolidated, and the freedoms of the American people. They also take task at solving the centuries-long complications caused by the Spirit Witch, that continually present themselves in modern day. Will Steven, Loraine, and the others ever get a reprieve from this seemingly endless fight? Will the Secret Society finally be defeated? Will

America survive the turmoil, and will the evil ones finally pay the debt for their crimes? All answers lie within the pages of the ongoing saga of the magical, mystical world of Branchview.

Follow Me – Brian Jay Nelson
Large Lion Entertainment

Website: branchview.info
Facebook: @infobranchview
Amazon @brianjaynelson

LIZZY MCNETT, BA
THINKER/WRITER/AUTHOR/PUBLISHER
Literary Agent/Publicist

PRESCOTT, ARIZONA
info@writerspublishinghouse.com
www.writerspubishinghouse.com

Chosen by God – The Little Brown One

Written by Willie Frances Hill

Book Review

Chosen by God - The Little Brown One delivers a gripping account of the life of Willie Frances Hill in a way that captures the reader from the very first chapter. The level of raw honesty and transparency is as refreshing as it is heart-wrenching. This book takes you on a roller coaster ride and does not let up until the very end.

I was entranced by the author's openness and in awe of her determination and strength as I read her story. With all the challenges and obstacles she encountered, she always held on to her faith in God even when it seemed she was too far gone. Her fierce tenacity to keep her family intact despite everything that was going on around her or the choices that she made was astonishing. Her longing for her mother's love that was never given and watching that scenario repeat throughout her family was so relatable. The author poured out her truth and laid it bare for all to see with the intention to show that she was "Chosen by God" and how all these life experiences helped her grow into the woman she became.

This book is a shining and powerful example for people of all faiths with a message to hod on to God and never give up no matter how dark the night may appear. Because when you are "Chosen by God," He will keep you through it all - alcoholism lust, bad decisions, sickness, violence, pain, loss of loved ones - Ms. Hill endured it all and tells this story as a living testament to her faith in God.

Chosen by God – The Little Brown One delivers a gripping account of the life of Willie Frances Hill

Author
WILLIE FRANCES HILL

*.... retired from Northrop Grumman.
She was an Analyst for 27 years.*

*After a few years of retirement, she wrote her first
novel "Chosen by God" The Little Brown One.
She was abandoned at seven along with her
sister who was nine.*

*Their mother left them with her estranged boyfriend
who they named the Giant. They were abused
and endured harsh whipping.*

They were forced to go to church so the giant could have his women over. This is where Willie was introduced to God and His goodness and mercy. This was a life changing moment, nothing was different at home, but she knew something had transformed her from the young girl of 12 to the matured 12years old who had power that gave her strength to leave after a beating to her sister from the giant. They left hitch hiking across town to find their mother to see if she could keep them. Having 2 more sibling, she said yes, someone to wash dirty diapers and care for her children.

At fifteen, Willie was forced to marry after getting pregnant with Joe who was 9 years older. Having 2 beautiful children. Later having her third child after leaving the marriage. She struggled caring for her children but persevered and provided a good life for her children grandchildren, sisters and their children. She had a village to care for. Willie worked various jobs to accomplish her mission. She started her career in Aero Space with Teledyne, Litton and retiring at Northrop Grumman.

JAMILAJAYPLUSSIZECASTING
Plus Size
CASTING
JAMILAJAYPlusSizeCasting.com
MODELING AGENCY, PLUS SIZE FASHION WEEK, PAGEANTS, REALITY SHOWS, FASHION SHOWS, COMMERCIALS, TELEVISION FEATURES & EXT
www.JAMILAJAYPLUSSIZECASTING.COM
JAMILAJAYPLUSSIZECASTING@GMAIL.COM

BRELEE

"A strong woman looks a challenge dead in the eye and gives it a wink." #breleeng

AUSTIN ,TEXAS

DRESS SIZE: 24
HEIGHT: 5'4
BUST: 44
CUP: DDD
HIPS: 51
WAIST: 39

Credit Tips During a Pandemic

Chayo Briggs, Credit King

The coronavirus outbreak could threaten your credit if you don't use your cards wisely. You'll want to avoid making some of these mistakes with your credit cards:

Taking on too much debt. Americans flocked to big-box chains and grocery stores to stock up on household staples and medications for COVID-19 quarantines. "It's likely consumers didn't worry about their balances and added to their credit card debt in order to stock up and protect their families," Allec says. But beware the risk of running up credit card debt.

Your credit score may drop, and you could pay interest charges if you carry a balance. You can control your credit card balance during the coronavirus threat if you: Stick to shopping lists. Check which supplies you have, and make a list of what you need. Buy only these items, and try to avoid stress purchases. Pay off card balances if possible.

If you charge coronavirus supplies on your credit card, aim to pay off your card balance before interest charges apply. Use your credit card rewards. You may be able to redeem points as a statement credit toward emergency purchases or redeem them for gift cards at stores where you can buy supplies.

Tap your emergency savings. The spread of COVID-19 is, after all, not just a national emergency but also a global health crisis. If you need to dip into your emergency savings to cover supplies, then take only what you need and plan to replenish the funds.

Missing payments. If you're facing financial hardship, reach out to your card issuer before you miss a payment. Ask if your issuer can be flexible with monthly payments and APRs. But also double-check that you won't have to make up any waived payments and fees.

You can control your credit card balance during the coronavirus threat if you:
Stick to shopping lists. Check which supplies you have, and make a list of what you need. Buy only these items, and try to avoid stress purchases.

Pay off card balances if possible. If you charge coronavirus supplies on your credit card, aim to pay off your card balance before interest charges apply.

Use your credit card rewards. You may be able to redeem points as a statement credit toward emergency purchases or redeem them for gift cards at stores where you can buy supplies.

Tap your emergency savings. The spread of COVID-19 is, after all, not just a national emergency but also a global health crisis. If you need to dip into your emergency savings to cover supplies, then take only what you need and plan to replenish the funds.

Missing payments. If you're facing financial hardship, reach out to your card issuer before you miss a payment. Ask if your issuer can be flexible with monthly payments and APRs. But also double-check that you won't have to make up any waived payments and fees.

A Financial Burdens During a Pandemic

Are you one of the many Americans carrying a large amount of credit debt? In the past credit scores have played a large part in determining the interest rates or terms of a loan when someone is applying for a loan or credit card. However, with the new FICO 10 score model announced in January 2020, it may have a huge impact on your credit rating.

Since 2008 credit card debt has continued to rise substantially. At the end of last year, according to Make it, "the number landed at about 13.95 trillion average." John Ulzheimer, a credit expert says, "this is bound to happen. The job of scoring models is to properly assess risk, not simply give people better scores as a default position."

FICO built the new score model using scoring from the big three credit bureaus agencies (Experian, TransUnion Equifax). The model will take effect by the end of 2020. In this new plan, certain criteria will affect scores, one being late payments and high debt that runs every month. Experts say it can lower score by as much as 20 points. The current credit suit had been consistent with no changes since 2014 when FICO released model 9. But this is the most meaningful change in many years. Although FICO 10 T is one variant that expands beyond old versions because it has a goal of giving lenders a more precise assessment of credit risk.

In the digital age, having a good credit resume is highly important. Intelligent technology allows for a more precise accounting of user's activities online and offline. FICO wanted a model for lenders to get a better way of analyzing trending data on a potential borrower's applications. The information would track history for twenty-four months in this, it creates a picture of your financial situation over time. In the FICO 10 scoring model, it focuses on the impact of late payments, causing a profound effect on the scoring results.

The new scoring model could potentially affect 110 million consumers. "Those consumers with recent delinquency or high utilization are likely going to see a downward shift and depending on the severity and recency of the delinquency it could be significant," Dave Shellenberger, FICO vice president of product management, said in a statement.

Despite, however, the changes will not occur immediately, because credit scoring happens overtime. Plus, the lender or banks have the option of which model they chose to use when deciding on a borrower's status.

In the new models trending data will include your balances, minimum payment amounts, plus the amount paid over the past twenty-four months. The analysis shows who pays their debt each month from the ones who make just the monthly payment. Along with the other results, the data will also determine if the consumer is reducing the debt, maintaining or increasing over time. The factors are better in predicting credit risk. Most consumers will also see added benefits for paying off the debt, besides lower interest rates.

But don't be fooled, delinquencies hurt more than just credit reports. If by chance someone is more than thirty days late on a payment the lender will generally report these late payments, which will harm your credit score.

One other area that may lower a FICO score is on personal loans. In the new model, a debt consolidation loan maybe even more beneficial than in the past, as certain high-risk consumers will be seen as a better credit risk. The focus is trying to stop consumers who use debt consolidation to pay off high-interest credit cards, then go right back and purchase high ticket items, increasing their newly paid debt. According to FICO, "By adopting the FICO® Score 10 Suite, a lender could reduce the number of defaults in their portfolio by as much as ten percent among newly originated bankcards and nine percent among newly originated auto loans, compared to using FICO® Score 9. The reduction in defaults is even higher for newly originated mortgage loans, at 17 percent compared to the version of the FICO Score used in that industry. These improvements in predictive power can help lenders safely avoid unexpected credit risk and better control default rates, while making more competitive credit offers to more consumers."

Credit experts, nonetheless suggest the best way to alleviate credit worry, is to practice good credit habits. "And while credit scores have been rising overall, FICO says almost half of U.S. adults either have low scores or no score whatsoever, so there's still a lot of room for improvement," said Ted Rossman, industry analyst at CreditCards.com.

CORONAVIRUS

SCAMMERS BEWARE!

How to avoid commerce scams:

Cybercriminals may take advantage of your need to self-quarantine to scam you out of your money. Most scams are "related to safety products and hard-to-find household goods," says Michael Lai, CEO of consumer-advocacy review service SiteJabber.com, which was initially funded by the U.S. National Science Foundation.

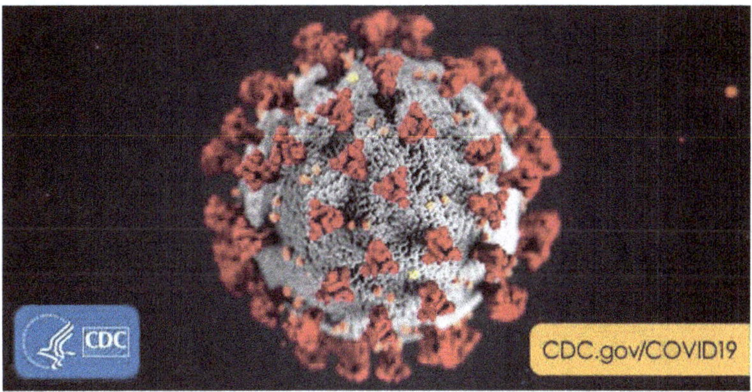

Currently, most of the complaints being submitted by shoppers to SiteJabber revolve around the travel industry, as people are discovering that travel insurance claims from certain providers may not be applicable for people who are stuck overseas or may need to cancel upcoming travel plans.

We are starting to see some consumer complaints about sites selling emergency preparedness materials where credit cards are charged, but nothing is delivered," Lai shares.

"We are also seeing a lot of complaints of price gouging as desperate consumers are resorting to unknown businesses to purchase things they can no longer find in local stores or even on Amazon." In particular, items like face masks, hand sanitizer, and gloves are being called out in these reviews, Lai says.

If you're shopping online, there may be certain advertisements in your inbox or in your social media feed that could be targeting you, Bischoff says. "If something seems too good to be true, it probably is," he explains, adding that unusually low prices and extraordinary claims are tip offs that an unknown retailer may not be reliable. Follow these tips to ensure your purchase is as legitimate as possible: Look for 'HTTPS': The lack of this established URL domain descriptor may be a signal that the site you are shopping on is compromised, Bischoff says, although some advanced scammers may use sites with 'https' as well.

Look for spelling errors: This is the most common sign that something is amiss. "Missing contact information is also another red flag, and no 'about' pages can be signs that you're browsing a scam site," Bischoff says. Always inspect the URL itself for misspelled words, which could be a dead giveaway.

Look for subdomains: As an example, amazon.store.com is much different than amazon.com, Bischoff explains. Always check the domain in your browser's URL, as most reputable retailers usually do not have an elaborate subdomain in their web address. Look for merchant reviews: Many retailers will have an official review system for customers to use on their sites, and you should be able to access product reviews or merchant feedback ratings before checking out. "If you're purchasing something on a marketplace like Amazon or eBay, never contact sellers or make payments outside of those marketplaces' official channels," Bischoff says.